Love You To Bits

By J. Boote

CONTENTS

Chapter 1

Davie Simpson hated it, on pure ethics, but even so, he had to admit it made him horny as fuck and this was where the problem lay. The problem also lay on his bedsheet because every time he had the dream he ended up rolling around in a puddle of his own cum all night.

It was a recurring dream as well—some would say a nightmare, but Davie would have to disagree. Not that he was going to tell anyone anyway, so he figured there had to be some kind of significance to it. Exactly what, though, he had no idea. He supposed that if he went to one of those child psychologists his mother, Jessica, occasionally threatened him with, that person might even suggest it was normal. Puberty did that to kids. The mother figure simply represented his confused feelings towards women and girls in general. Davie would tell her that was bullshit. Because fucking with his mother every night when he went to bed was not his idea of confusion, when he woke up it was his idea of sick and perverted. He could have dreamt about screwing with Jenny from his class, maybe Sarah the neighbour, but no, it had to be his mother whose lips were clamped around his cock. Among other things.

It started soon after he had his first ever orgasm a couple of weeks ago. He knew of some kids who were jerking off at the age of twelve or thirteen and he had no idea what they were really talking about when smirking and joking to each other. He'd watched the same porn channels as they did on his laptop but felt nothing. In one of his friend's home, he had watched while some girl was roughly fucked up the arse by something that resembled the size of Davie's arm while

4

another grabbed her by the hair with both hands and fucked her mouth. As an added detail which Davie found mildly disgusting and imagined had to be pretty damn painful was another woman with her fist up the girl's pussy, ramming it in and out like a piston. When Davie looked at his own meagre offerings in private, he thought he might be in a lot of trouble. If girls liked to be fucked by something resembling the thickness of a large branch there was a good chance he may remain a virgin the rest of his life.

And yet, at just shy of his fourteenth birthday, while watching such a movie (this time just a girl sucking off someone's dick until she got a face full) his dick had magically grown double its size and while messing around with it, he had inadvertently sprayed his laptop screen unable to stop himself. Not that he had wanted to but the clean-up operation afterwards had been messy and gross. If his parents caught him or asked why the screen was suddenly smeared and he told the truth, they'd lock him in the basement for a week. His parents, especially his mother, were very religious.

Normally, he would have been shocked and disgusted. While it was true that some of his friends at school had some pretty hot-looking mothers, this was not the case with Davie's. Yes, she had a pretty good figure for a forty-year-old, but there it stopped. Her skin was blotchy, her lips thin like a scar, eyes green and menacing, so that anyone who happened to catch her eye quickly looked away. She never wore makeup which made her look even older and her hair was black and cut short, almost a crewcut. Because she barely wore dresses or skirts—couldn't possibly reveal any more skin than necessary to the locals—she was often mistaken for a man. And Davie often thought that was the look she was going for, always wearing sensible clothing, men's shoes. What his father had seen in her he could never imagine.

In his dream, though, none of this mattered. The dream always started the same. He was in church sitting at the back with his mother, everyone singing and praying. This time it was his father the priest and for some reason he was completely naked except for a large, long crucifix around his neck and a raging hard-on that he balanced his bible on while reciting. This part always had Davie laughing at the sheer stupidity of it. But then, his mother, with a twinkle in her green eye and a leery, suspicious smile on her face, started caressing the inside of his leg while whispering in his ear how beautiful he was. This alone was enough to cause his cock to stiffen. It dwindled slightly when she poked a double-pointed tongue like a serpent's in his ear and began slurping his ear wax, but her fingers now gripping his cock tight in her hand counteracted it.

"Get undressed," she whispered in his ear, in that of a man's voice, deep and raucous like an old man. As though under her spell, without question he rose and pulled down his trousers and underwear, his cock springing out from tight confines like a soldier standing to attention. It was huge too, now resembling those guys on the porn video. His father continued lecturing on the evils of sin, completely ignoring him as though he wasn't there. Then, his mother stood and tore off her blouse, her huge breasts like deflating balloons, nipples like bullets, then tore off her dress, revealing nothing underneath. Her pubic hair was shaped into that of a cross, yet upside-down, perhaps a mockery of what her husband and Davie's father was currently lecturing about. Davie could smell the muskiness of her already, juices running down her leg, forming a small puddle on the wooden floor.

"That's my holy water, son, drink."

Again, without hesitation, Davie knelt down, as though about to pray, and lapped it up like a dog. It tasted like blood, which wasn't surprising as apparently it was her time of the month and blood was mingled with it. It only made Davie's cock throb harder rather than disgust him. When he'd finished licking it all up, he sat down again. She leaned over and stuck her serpentine tongue in his mouth that went right to the back of his throat making him gag.

"Now fuck me in God's house. Hurt me."

She turned around and bent over so much her head was now between her legs like she was about to lick her own pussy. Without a second thought and feeling like he was about to fuck the hottest woman on Earth, Davie lunged, almost knocking her over with the force of entry. In her arse, of course, because she insisted it be that way. Jessica screamed as he entered her, yet as if by magic or a spell, no one else in the church heard her. Everyone in the rows before them acted as if nothing had happened, Davie's father now reciting some psalm Davie had no idea about but mentioned the devil's seed. And in this dream, Davie's cock had grown substantially, wider too, almost as thick as his wrist. The skin and flesh around Jessica's arsehole tore and ripped like someone tearing a piece of fabric. And he continued fucking her, her head banging against her own legs while she did indeed lick and fist-fuck herself until he pulled out his cock, stuck it in her mouth and howled as he came in the back of her throat.

He guessed it was probably around this time he did the same thing in his bed. Pretty logical, he thought, considering. Then, the funniest part, was as they both dressed again, cum running from Jessica's nostrils and down her chin, everyone turned around and clapped as if they'd been aware this whole time but had wanted to give them some privacy. Even Mike, Davie's dad, cheered and clapped, with his own cock swinging from side to side like a metronome.

It was at this point that Jessica turned to face her son and her eyes were wild and red orbs, no whites showing at all as if the blood had rushed to her head and filled her sockets as well. That was when Davie, on the verge of screaming, woke up, in a sweat and cum drenched bed.

It may have continued this way for a while, until Davie found himself a proper girlfriend but it was something else that changed everyone's fate. He came home from school one day to find his mother waiting for him, hands on her hips, looking like she was on the verge of throwing up or was going to kill him. Maybe both.

"You dirty, disgusting little pig, you," she spat at him.

"What? What have I done?"

"What have you done? You're filthy. A disgusting, filthy, sinful child. How dare you be a son of mine? You were spawned by the devil, you horrid little monster."

"What are you talking about? I haven't done anything!"

"Come with me."

She grabbed him by the earlobe and dragged him upstairs, Davie wincing, wondering what the hell she had discovered now. His porn mags? Had been checking the history on his laptop? But that had a password.

She dragged him into the bedroom and pointed at the sheets. There was a big stain in the middle and then he knew.

"What have you been doing, you sinful child? You disgust me! You keep doing that, it will fall off, did you know that? Maybe I should cut it off, teach you a lesson."

Davie had nothing to say. What could he say? He thought it was perfectly normal. Maybe not the fucking his mother part in his dream, but otherwise?

She slapped his face, hard. Then grabbed him by the arm and dragged him back downstairs. She stopped at the basement door, threw it open and pushed him down.

"You can stay down there tonight, heathen, foul pig. Think about what you did. There's a bible to keep you company. I suggest you read it."

Jessica slammed the door shut and locked it. Davie was going to remain down there all night without food or water. And if he wanted a piss or worse he'd have to do it on the floor. It was in that moment that he decided things were going to change. Things had to stop and seeing his mother's demonic, red orbs for eyes gave him an idea.

Chapter 2

Davie had once heard a story about a guy who lived not too far away in nearby Bradwell. According to local legend, he had been sacked as a fireman due to budget cuts and hadn't taken it well. The looming threat of losing his home through not being able to pay the mortgage meant he had taken some pretty drastic measures. Through a combination of rage, hate and the need for revenge, he had somehow managed to summon a demon. One that he used to kill his boss by reducing him almost completely to ash, so that he looked like a victim of either spontaneous combustion or someone had burned his body at a temperature so high only ash remained and he had then transported the body to his deceased boss's home.

Exactly what happened afterwards was never entirely clarified, except that he was found dead in the exact same circumstances, this time his ten-year-old son who watched him burn alive until nothing remained except a partial, charred foot and part of his face. Following this, though, several more people died, burnt to ashes and the true killer was never caught. But one enterprising person who had followed the case closely had suggested the possibility that one or more of those involved may have been a subject of demonic possession. The fact no one was ever caught and that the deaths were so horrific and bizarre was more than enough for this person to spread dark whispers and rumours around the village. He even gave the demon a name—Xaphan, keeper of the fires of Hell.

This was not lost on Davie as he sat at his laptop that night, after spending the previous in the basement, having to crush or swipe away the assorted bugs and spiders that lived down there. After letting him out, then telling him to go shower and scrub himself with soap until his skin bled, his mother hadn't said a word to him when he left for school. He figured the lecture would come that night when his father was home from school, but for some reason it never came. He assumed they were discussing in private how to punish him or teach him a lesson. Well now, if things went right, it was going to be her that learned a lesson, a very hard and painful one.

Literally.

And the kind of demon he wanted to summon was the kind that would teach her what cardinal sin and the devil's seed was all about. Feigning interest in an English project, he had spoken to his Religious Studies teacher, pretending that he wanted to write an essay on demonic possession after seeing a movie he had enjoyed. He had asked what types of demons there were, if Xaphan really was the supposed demon of fire and he had been surprised when his teacher said yes, that each demon had a specific function. Not wanting to raise any suspicions, although conscious that it was probably a typical question from a horny fifteen-year-old, he had then asked him about demons related to fertility and procreation. The teacher smiled and gave him a name.

"So how would one summon this demon or whatever it's called?" he asked pretending to sound stupid, yet his heart thudding in his chest, anxiety and excitement almost giving him a hard-on just thinking about it.

The teacher told him.

Now, Davie sat staring at his laptop browsing through various dark web sites his friend had told him about. Ones that were supposed to be true, not some fake shit a scammer had invented. And there it was. The demon known as Asmodeus glared back at him with its monstrous face, spiralled, dangerous looking horns on his head and between his legs, something no less dangerous. Something that would split his bitch of a mother in two. And that was just what he was looking for. Fuck her and her carnal sins, she was going to know what it was like to fuck with him.

In more ways than one.

To summon the creature wasn't as difficult as he thought it would be. He'd had visions of having to sacrifice a new-born baby, perhaps a cat or something while invoking the demon, but it was much easier than that. It might even be enjoyable, he thought, as he pulled down his trousers and began to massage his already throbbing cock.

Davie began to recite the passage while simultaneously jerking off. This was imperative, apparently, so that Asmodeus could sense his lust, his desires, helping to bring him closer to his world. He finished reciting the long passage then began to repeat the same as instructed. A good sense of timing was going to be required here as well so he didn't cum too soon. He tried to conjure an image of his mother naked, to ward off such a thing but this only made things worse. But it didn't matter anyway. As he started reciting the invocation again, the room darkened. The air crackled with static. A musty smell filled the room, salty, and he knew from experience what that was.

Then, as if by magic, which in a way he supposed it

was, the image on the laptop changed. *Moved.* As though from a great distance he could hear wailing, howling, mingled with a deep, raucous chuckle that rumbled and roared in his head. Asmodeus, whose image he had been jerking off to on the screen came to life and now instead of just his head and the upper half of his body Davie could see all of it. His religious teacher hadn't been joking when he said this was the demon of lust.

The thing that had been between his legs had been vertical, standing to attention. Now that he could see the creature's whole body the rest of its monstrosities were revealed. Davie saw four enormous, black, furry cocks throbbing with fury, huge and thick like Davie's arms. As Asmodeus turned to face the flock that surrounded him, Davie saw two thick appendages on the front, two behind him, so he could easily fuck four people at once, back and forth, back and forth. A constant drizzle of pre-cum dripped from each head.

Davie stopped mid-sentence as the image took on a clearer aspect. People were lining up, screaming and sobbing. They were naked, the men with erections, slapping at their cocks to—Davie assumed—make it go away. The moment Davie stopped chanting, a sudden stabbing to his head almost made him scream out in agony, as if a piece of his skull had broken off and lodged itself onto the grey matter. Asmodeus was looking directly at him and he knew what he wanted— keep reciting the passage. Davie did so.

Then, those first in the queues turned around and bent over, spreading their legs and their arse cheeks and slowly backed onto one of the demon's dripping cocks. Asmodeus thrust into them, four at once, the tip of his cock going straight up and out their mouths as he pumped them, like a cuckoo popping in and out of a cuckoo clock as the hour struck. Gargled screams and howls of pain came from the victims, both men and women, Asmodeus roaring with lust while Davie somehow managed to continue reciting. His orders, for it to work, were to repeat again and again until told to stop. He would know when it was time to stop. Davie's mouth was very dry but he didn't dare pause to grab a drink or anything. Only now was the pain in his brain subsiding.

Asmodeus continued fucking the souls of the condemned as Davie understood them to be until his whole, massive body began to shake and tremble, as did the bodies of his victims. Then, in one gargantuan roar that even made Davie's laptop shake and for Davie to cover his ears, the creature pulled out each cock and showered the souls in his thick cum. But still their torture wasn't complete.

As thick wads of cum rained down on each soul, as though buckets of saliva were being poured onto them, the cum began to sizzle. Smoke first rose in wisps then shortly after bellowed as the cum melted through their flesh and bone like acid leaving them a messy, jellified blob on the floor, the stench so foul and strong Davie could smell it. The stench of burnt, rotting flesh and hair that seemed to drift through the screen somehow and fill his room. Barely able to chant above a mumble, Davie continued, now too terrified to stop, and was even more shocked when the jellied blobs on the floor slowly began to grow again until they were perfectly formed human beings. They then went to the back of the queue and waited for the same process to be repeated while the next four hapless victims bent over.

This process continued another four times—souls in a perpetual state of being fucked to death—when Davie felt his body start tingling. He was still jerking off, his hand aching by now, surprised he hadn't come himself yet, although the horrific scenes he had just witnessed may have contributed to that. He rose from the chair as though commanded; someone having taken over his mind and spirit. It was harder to breathe, his body felt lighter, his cock as though every single nerve in his body ended right at the tip. He was going to explode in lust and carnal excitement, never having felt so good before. His heart was going to explode, his head, his cock. Something, as though he was being wrapped in a tight shroud smothered his body, Asmodeus drawing closer to the screen so Davie could see his own reflection in the demon's many eyes. His mouth opened revealing multiple rows of triangular shaped teeth like a shark, a tongue red and throbbing but was actually a penis darting in and out like a snake and then a voice in Davie's mind roared at him to finish while reciting the final paragraph in the invocation.

He did so and in the exact moment of saying the last word Davie's cock did explode, showering the screen in his cum but somehow traversing the screen and going straight into the demon's mouth and down his throat. He wasn't sure if he screamed in that moment through sheer ecstasy and prayed he hadn't. The idea was that Asmodeus was going to take over his mother's soul and condemn her to perpetual suffering and carnal torment for all eternity but the way he was feeling now, as though something had inhabited and taken over his own body made him wonder. Even so, now terribly tired and not feeling well at all, he turned off the laptop and crawled into bed. His dreams that night, while not involving his mother, were still turbulent and crude.

Chapter 3

Jessica hadn't been feeling herself for a while now. She was prone to headaches which, of course, was God punishing her for past sins. Exactly what those sins were she wasn't entirely sure but something she had done to upset Him, and this was the consequence. Although the more she thought about it, she had an idea what that sin might have been. She'd spoken about it with her husband, Mike, but he was weak-minded, not strong as God would have wanted. Even though he bore a look of disgust on his face, he had tried to tell her it was normal behaviour for boys.

Normal behaviour? It was disgusting, filthy behaviour. It said so in the bible. Davie would go to hell for what he had done and was doing and something had to be done to prevent it. She had suggested that he be left in the basement for a week with barely any food or water to cleanse his soul, let himself become purified like God's holy water but when Mike had hinted that they might be arrested for such an act, she had backed down. Something about human rights. Well, Davie had no right behaving in that manner in her own home. He was a demon, a monster, uncouth and sick. She'd been sick herself after throwing away the tainted bedsheets then, not happy with that, burning them in the back garden, all the time reciting from the bible praying for forgiveness for what Davie had done. It might technically be against the law to lock her son in the basement for a week, but she was going to make damn sure he was adequately punished. Maybe she should make him scrub it with sandpaper until it bled. Maybe she should whip him, right there on his thing, just as

Jesus was whipped. That would make him think twice.

So yes, now she thought she knew what sin she had committed. She had allowed herself to be pollinated by a man. Had succumbed to dark desires and irrational thought, allowed herself to be taken and impaled, his filthy seed remaining in her body until she was with child. If only she hadn't been so weak that night, had kept her legs closed. Perhaps she should have flayed Mike just as she was planning on doing to Davie. He should have been castrated! When they decided on marriage the decision should have been made there and then, go to a private doctor and have him remove the foul, ghastly thing. The Devil's organ. Satan's sperm. Curse of all mankind.

When Davie had gone to school earlier she had rushed up to check his sheets again, daring him to have soiled the sheets once more, but this time they were clean, not a hint of any uncouth behaviour. His laptop had been open, though, and when she messed around with the keys trying to get it to fire up, see if any filth was on that too, there had been a sudden flash. The room had darkened, the air heavy and oppressive, and something had appeared on the screen. A creature, she thought, with multiple eyes like a spider, sly grin on a wicked, inhuman face, both hands shaking frantically below the screen. She realised with horror what the thing was doing but then her mind had gone blank, and the next thing she knew she was lying on the floor of the living room completely naked.

Jessica sat up shocked, quickly closing the curtains to avoid further embarrassment. Good job Davie was at school and Mike at work, or she would have had to lock herself in the basement for a week, never mind her son.

Her clothes were beside her so she dressed again, wondering what on earth could have happened for her to be lying there this way. It was blasphemous, maybe she should go to church and confess again, seek advice from the vicar. She needed to pray for forgiveness again. Because something was very wrong.

As she dressed, she noticed the insides of her thighs were wet. There was a musty smell in the air, not unlike Davie's bedroom yesterday morning. And as she pulled up her no-nonsense knickers, she found her fingers lingering just a little too long over the thick bush that hid her poison. As if controlled by outside forces, her fingers started tickling the slit between the bush, and she had to forcefully pull her hand away with her other to avoid them slipping in. She sobbed in disgust and horror, incapable of understanding where such a disgusting idea could have come from. Her brain was being filled with filthy, alien thoughts. As she put her bra on, her fingers inadvertently brushed her nipples and they were hard as rocks, tingling as she touched them. She shrieked, rapidly putting on her blouse. When she stepped away she realised there was a throbbing between her legs, much like after that time Davie had been conceived. She shrieked again.

"What the fuck is wrong with me?!" she yelled at the empty house then screamed and slapped a hand over her mouth after hearing that obscene word come from her lips. Jessica never swore, and neither did anyone in her close proximity. The one time she had heard Davie say a foul word she had dragged him to the bathroom, forced him to open his mouth then shoved a bar of soap in there, telling him to scrub his mouth out until it bled. After he vomited, she made him clean that

19

up too with his bare hands.

The devil had gotten to her. He must have done. She hadn't prayed hard enough during her life and now God had forsaken her, left her to the devil to do as he pleased. She rushed upstairs to the toilet, needing to clean the dirty area between her legs. She sat on the toilet, urinating first, sobbing as she did so, feeling dirty and repulsed inside. When she stood up and turned to flush the toilet, she staggered back and clamped a hand over her mouth again. The bowl was red, a dark thick liquid swishing around in there, running down the sides. Things moved in the gore-filled bowl, tiny things like maggots or worms and when she peered closer to see what it was, a scream bubbling away at the back of her throat, it finally released when she saw what they were.

Not maggots, worms or bugs, but something even more horrific and alien. Dozens of tiny, hard penises wriggled around there as though imitating caterpillars. They even had hairy ball sacks attached to them and they were trying to crawl up the sides of the toilet bowl to get out. Where the slit should be, in the centre of the tip, was a tiny eyeball that blinked up at her, and she knew they were seeing her, staring right back at her. They managed to get so far up the bowl before dropping back into the bloody water and making splashes, squealing as they fell.

Jessica whimpered, shocked, unable to react. Somehow, in her mind, she could hear them talking to her, begging to be let out. Telling her she knew she wanted them. That if she saved and fed them with the cum of her husband and son they would grow into gargantuan monstrosities and would fulfil her every

20

desire. She clapped hands over her ears, trying to drown them out but if anything their voices echoed even louder.

And the worst part of everything was that she was oh so tempted to do so. She found herself bending over, a hand reaching down to scoop them up, nurse them to health, help them grow. She wanted to kiss each one like they were her baby pets, but through a force of willpower she didn't know she possessed she reached up and flushed the toilet instead. The things squealed as they swirled around in circles, before being dragged down to the sewers, their little eyeballs blinking rapidly. When she dared to look back, the toilet was perfectly clean as if nothing had happened and the wet area around the insides of her thighs was once again dry.

Jessica panted, trying to get her breath back. And her sanity, for it was clear she was quickly losing it. She needed to visit Reverend Wilson as fast as possible, then scrub herself until her skin was red raw. Her bible, she needed her bible. Where was it? In the drawer beside her bed, where it always was, so she could read before going off to sleep. She rushed to grab it, yet when she opened the drawer the bible was gone, replaced by something else, something diabolical. A book that looked as old as time itself lay there, on its cover two people in the throes of lust. A woman laying there with her ankles behind her ears and a man fucking her hard. She knew he was fucking her hard because the image was not a still image. It was as if she was looking at an iPad screen instead of a book, a porn scene being played out and the two were grunting and panting as he thrust harder and faster into her.

And the two people on the cover were her and Davie, both looking up at Jessica as they fucked, sly grins on their faces, eyes twinkling.

"Hey, Mum! You're a real good fuck, you know that? Why didn't you tell me? Your arse is so tight and wet. I got shit all over my cock and I love it! I'm gonna stick it in your mouth and let you suck it all off as I cum. That sound cool or what?"

She was openly crying now, unable to understand what was happening to her. Such filth, depraved and obscene. When she blinked and looked back again, her trusty bible was there as it had always been. She snatched it up and hugged it to her chest. Then threw it back on the bed when her nipples, still hard like rocks, tingled, causing another wet patch to form between her legs, a small puddle forming on the floor.

"Fuck me, Jesus, and I will be your whore for all eternity."

She shrieked. She hadn't just said that. She had imagined it. There was someone in her head, corrupting her mind and thoughts. She needed an exorcism. That or lock herself in a room at Northgate Hospital for the Mentally Impaired and never be released again. And it was Davie's fault; it had to be. Him and his obscenities, putting wicked thoughts in her head.

She'd take care of him after visiting with the priest. But first, she needed to lie down for a bit. She was tired, extremely so, and not surprising given the circumstances. But as soon as she closed her eyes, before she was even asleep, her mind was taken over and she found herself in another place. A dark, seedy place.

She was lying naked on a grave. When she turned to

see who's grave it was she was shocked to see it was her long-deceased mother's. She had died of cancer and they had prayed long and hard during the nights of excruciating pain, telling each other she would soon be by God's side. But now, it wasn't God who was by Jessica's side but Davie. He was naked too. Standing over her, grinning, licking his lips.

"Hi, Mummy. Wanna play?"

It was as if she was watching things through another's eyes, while at the same time firmly planted in her own naked body, sprawled there on her mother's grave, furiously rubbing her clit, unable to control herself. She desperately wanted to wake up from this nightmare, scream and run to the church, lock herself in and never leave, but another part of her wanted him.

"Yes, I do," she heard herself say.

She watched as he stroked his cock. A cock that was huge and thick and twitching in anticipation, throbbing and bobbing up and down, thick veins coiled around it, pulsating. Jessica thought of little Davie growing up, in more ways than one. How he had grown, become a man. Davie slowly squatted and directed his cock onto Jessica's face, teasing her as her tongue caressed the tip.

"Give it to me," she begged.

"Open wide now, Mother. And what do we say, first?"

"Our Lord, who art in heaven. Thy kingdom cum, when He is done. Give us this day our daily bread, our daily cock. Lead us into temptation and corruption. Drown thee in thy cum. And make me fucking squirm."

She opened her mouth wide and it was filled.

It kept filling until she was sure it was trying to push

through the walls of her pussy. She gagged, unable to help it, snot running from her nostrils as Davie began to pump in and out, his balls slapping against her forehead. He reached over and thrust his fist into her, twisting it around, opening and flexing his fingers, sharp fingernails raking her as though trying to claw her from the inside out. Part of her wanted to scream in horror, another in ecstasy.

Davie pulled out what felt like a truncheon in her mouth then stuck it into her pussy, grunting as he did so. Now it was the complete opposite, as if it was burrowing up past her throat, trying to break free.

"That feel good, Mother? It's what you always wanted, isn't it? That's why you had a son, so he could fuck when dad didn't want to. I fuck you on your mother's grave. Isn't that a movie or something?"

He thrust into her hard before she could reply. Now he was fucking her so hard she was banging her head against her mother's gravestone, almost causing it to topple over. He gripped her ankles and brought them up over her head, holding her down while he banged her, all the time grinning his boyish grin.

But then it changed. Suddenly it wasn't Davie anymore. His face morphed into something else. An insect/human hybrid. Eyes dotted all over his face like blisters. His lips cracked open, pus and some dark liquid running down his chin as his mouth grew wider, reaching his ears, showing sharp, pointed teeth that glistened. All the time he continued pumping into her and it felt as though his cock was growing too, about to split her open like a ripe fruit.

Jessica tried to scream, but something blocked her vocal cords, his cock maybe, because it felt as though it was right up there, playing tag with her throat. Then the ground beneath her began to tremble as though an earthquake was brewing, but this was England, earthquakes didn't happen here. She felt the earth around her give way as she sank a few inches, now terrified the ground was going to open up and she would fall into her mother's grave, be buried alive with her rotting, skeletal body.

Instead, two hands shot out and wrapped themselves around her, fumbling for something to grab onto. Davie laughed, now fucking so fast he became a blur. Two legs appeared beside her, the flesh hanging on in clumps, sinewy strings of muscle tissue dangling like earthworms. Bugs and cockroaches scurried across Jessica's body, into her mouth, down her throat. She bit down on several, feeling their bodies explode in her mouth and warm blood and intestines splattering the insides of her cheeks. In her horror, and with Davie's cock banging her harder and harder, making it almost impossible to breathe, she swallowed the cockroaches' innards. Davie laughed harder, his multiple eyes gleaming with delight, thick wads of spit dribbling down his face and plopping onto Jessica.

The ground opened up further and a head appeared, followed by a skeletal body, riddled with more bugs and worms. Jessica turned to look and was face to face with her dead mother who grinned at her, cockroaches running up what remained of her nose, in and out of her mouth, nibbling on the remains of her eyeballs.

"Having a good fuck, daughter?" she cackled. "You always were a little whore, weren't you? Pretending you didn't like it when Mike fucked you that night. You wanted more. You wanted it in your arse. Your dad fucked me on the church altar, got me pregnant with you so you're definitely God's daughter now. The vicar invited us all to fuck with him. Maybe you're his daughter, not your father's. I was fucked so many times that day, I nearly drowned in their holy cum. On your first birthday you were baptised with their cum, not holy water."

She cackled louder, like a diseased crow. Jessica would have howled at her, told her she was lying were it not for being rocked back and forth still, unable to catch her breath.

"And now you're gonna die from that same cum, you dirty, filthy little slut."

In that moment, Davie pulled out his cock, which felt as though she was having half her intestines removed at the same time, directed it at her naked body and showered her with thick jets of his cum that splashed onto her body and face. It seemed to never end, spurt after spurt as Davie roared and her mother cackled to the point she thought she was going to drown. Finally, he did stop, but not her suffering. As if his cum was laced with sugar or some sweet substance, the bugs and insects flocked. Soon her body was alive with assorted worms, cockroaches, and other nameless insects that began to swarm over her soaked body, eating up the sticky substance then continuing until they were gnawing at her soft, wet flesh. Jessica, pinned down, was unable to move and could only watch as her flesh was gradually eaten away, feel the bugs burrowing inside her, scurrying around and biting her intestines and organs. It was as if thousands of tiny blades were pricking at them, stabbing her multiple times. Two large cockroaches began nibling at her eyeballs, others ran up her nostrils and she was sure she could feel them chomping on her brain. Several rats, perhaps alerted by the smell or the commotion, ran over. One pushed its way up into her stretched pussy, its tail sticking out like an old tampon. Soon this was gnawing at the walls of her pussy too while the other began to chomp on her nipples, tearing them off and swallowing them before going back for more.

It continued this way for several minutes, while Davie and Jessica's mother cheered them on and Jessica's body slowly and magically disappeared, bite by bite. When only her skeleton remained and the last of her brain was being chewed upon, did Davie lean over and kiss her gently where her lips would have been. *Such a nice boy. He makes me so proud*, she thought as the world turned to darkness and suddenly she was sitting bolt upright in bed, her body soaked in sweat.

When she looked down at herself, she was covered in sweat and tiny bite marks, and there was a large wet stain between her legs where it throbbed like *that* night.

And when she turned to the bedroom door and saw Davie standing there, a look of amazement on her face, rather than be embarrassed and shocked, she wanted him inside her, right there and then. But instead, Davie grinned and left, gently closing the door behind him.

Chapter 4

Jessica opened her eyes and looked around. It was dark so at first assumed it was early in the morning. Yet Mike's side of the bed was empty and when she touched the pillow it was cold. So either he hadn't come home that night or it wasn't night time. She glanced at the digital clock beside her bed. It said 7:23. If it was that time in the morning there would be daylight streaming through the window already. Which meant…

She sat up, confused, trying to remember anything from the last few hours and found that she couldn't. Maybe she had been feeling ill and had wanted to lie down for a while, because now that she was waking fully, she realised she had a headache. Her whole body ached, in fact. Maybe a trip to the doctor was called for. The flu or something, the last thing she needed right now. Mike would be home from work in an hour or so and dinner needed preparing so she hauled herself out of bed and dragged herself to the landing. She swayed on her feet for a moment, strange images flashing through her mind. Something about her mother, but she had been deceased for years and, God forgive me, she thought, maybe it wasn't such a bad thing. Not a nice woman. She was about to head downstairs when she heard weird noises coming from Davie's room. She recalled what she found on his sheets the other day, and all ideas of feeling unwell were immediately dissipated.

She burst in, not bothering to knock and her suspicions were confirmed. Davie's laptop was open, as were his legs, his trousers around his ankles, and on the screen a mass orgy seemed to be underway, legs and bodies everywhere, panting and groaning loud and clear.

"You dirty, filthy creature," she gasped. "What did I tell you about doing that, you sinful, vile person?"

But Davie didn't even look ashamed or embarrassed. In fact, he carried on jerking off in front of his mother, a big, silly smirk on his face.

If she had been carrying a knife with her she might have ran over and sliced it off for him, teach him a proper lesson, but instead, she burst over to where he was sitting and swiped his hand away. She then brought back her hand, ready to slap him across the face repeatedly, and then he was going into the basement for a week, child abuse or not. But, the moment she slapped his hand away from the still throbbing organ, she had inadvertently touched it and something had happened in her mind. Immediately, all rage and thoughts of punishment vanished, to be replaced by something she had not known in years, if ever—lust. It was as if her mind was clouded over, or someone else had taken possession of it, some telepathic trick, because now, the feelings she had towards the scene before her were the complete opposite.

She glanced back at the screen. A woman was straddling one guy while another was fucking her at the same time, yet another his cock in her mouth and this was single-handedly the most erotic, exciting thing she had ever witnessed. She wanted to be that woman. But knowing that was highly unlikely right now, she did the next best thing, Davie as though he were a stranger she had never met before. She squatted, swatted away his hand and took his cock in hers.

"Is that better? Is that what you really wanted?"

"Yes, it is. You know what to do. Do it."

His voice was the huskiest, sexiest voice on Earth and she was powerless to resist. Slowly at first, she squeezed then began to pump his throbbing organ, looking him in the eyes while doing so, revelling in what she was doing. Jessica lowered her head and licked it, now moving her hand faster while rubbing her tongue over it. It didn't take long before Davie started groaning, arching his back, and before she knew it, her hand and arm was covered in his sticky mess.

It was in that very second that she looked into his eyes again, then at what was now a deflating organ in her hand and she was herself once more, her own son sitting there who she had just perverted.

A whimper escaped her. Her face contorted into something that has just witnessed the most despicable act imaginable. She could feel the muscles on her face contort and twist. Davie leered back at her, chuckling. She looked at the slime on her hand and arm and whimpered again, as though acid had just been poured onto it. Repulsion sweeping through her, she stood up and wiped her hand and arm on Davie's still-smirking face, then snapped closed the laptop.

"Dear God, forgive me my sins. Whatever it is I did to offend thee, punish me but stop this devil child from sinning further."

Then she slapped him across the face. "Come with me, devil-child. This stops now. You have a demon inside you. A devil has corrupted your soul and we need to stop it from possessing you further. I'll make it stop before it's too late."

She dragged him towards the bathroom, his trousers and underwear still around his ankles, almost causing him to trip. He said nothing as she led him away and she could only hope and pray it was because he was too ashamed to do so. When she reached the bathroom she made him bend over the bathtub.

"The devil has carnal desires, we have to stop him getting in. From penetrating our bodies. And aside from prayer, which you will be doing lots of from now on, we have to use other means as well."

Jessica opened the cabinet on the wall next to her and pulled out a small box. She opened it, fumbled with the wrapper then with one hand spread Davie's arse cheeks apart while with the other she pushed the tampon up inside.

"There, that will stop Satan getting in. It's how he does it, you know. Fornication is the greatest of sins and so he uses the openings on man and woman to creep in. I'll do the same myself tonight after I have prayed. Your father has been doing it since you were conceived. Now, pull your trousers up and follow me."

Again, saying nothing, Davie did as he was told and followed after his mother. They headed downstairs where she threw open the basement door and waited for him to enter. He did so without argument.

"Now, I want you to think about what you did. Read the bible, repent and pray for forgiveness. We can only pray God will listen this time and stop this immoral, sick behaviour of yours. When you think you've learned your lesson or that God has forgiven you, we will see."

And with that she slammed the door shut and locked it, sighing to herself and shaking her head. Mike's dinner needed cooking still. So much to do, so much sin in the world.

31

Chapter 5

Things hadn't quite turned out as Davie expected them to. According to what he had read on the link, the demon should have transferred itself to whoever Davie commanded it to, then immediately taken over her body. And while at first he had been hopeful it had worked, now he wasn't so sure. Yes, he had been more than shocked when after the initial horror at seeing him jerk off earlier, she had decided to take matters into her own hand. But once he had come, there had been another transformation. Back to her usual pathetic naïve self. He thought she was going to get undressed and run naked through the streets or something, fuck anything and everything she could grab hold of, but no, it hadn't worked that way at all.

And now here he was stuck in this fucking basement again, no doubt all night and for a few days after that as well. As his mother dragged him down here his mind had been reeling thinking it had all gone wrong and now she was going to make him suffer like never before, but now, thinking about it, maybe, just maybe he had been wrong.

Because it had been in that instant when she had changed back again, he had noticed the transition. That creature's face appeared in his mind except it wasn't in his mind; it was as though he *was* that creature. An immense surge of lust had exploded in his body just as he had exploded over his mother's hand. He would have taken her there and then and fucked her for a thousand years if she hadn't changed back. He would have fucked anyone for a thousand years, the fucking dog if it was still alive. Now, his whole body belonged to another. He was a walking, breathing hormone desperate to stick his already stiff cock into someone again. He would fuck himself if that was technically possible.

And it wasn't just this desire that raged through him, either. Other things he was aware of. Even though she was upstairs he could hear her thoughts, read her mind. Right now, she was praying for forgiveness, kneeling beside her bed. If he wanted to he could break down the door just by thought alone, grab her by the hair and tear her head off with his bare hands.

But that would be too easy. Far too easy.

For both of them.

For while his dad was barely home, away all day at work, he was just as bad as she was. Scared of her like a coward, allowing himself to be ordered about, not forcing himself upon her to fulfil his needs. But, like the tank of a car slowly being filled with fuel, so was he slowly being fuelled, with power and abilities he could never have dreamed off. By tomorrow, when he was fully charged, nothing and no one was going to stop him.

To test out his newfound abilities, he rose and looked up at the ceiling. Spiders dangled there like crude decorations. Big, fat ones too. Davie took a deep breath and scurried up the wall, imitating the bugs and spiders. When he reached the ceiling he crawled along it and grabbed one of the spiders. He popped it into his mouth and chewed on it slowly, its innards exploding in his mouth as its legs tickled his cheeks while frantically trying to scurry away. He chuckled to himself imagining all the things he could do. Swallowing the spider he crawled to the other side and scurried down the wall again. His balls were going to burst if he didn't do something about it. If he jerked off now it would be Niagara Falls spurting from his cock. But jerking off was boring. He considered breaking down the door and going after his mother but forced himself to stick to his plan. Instead, he searched around the barely lit, almost empty basement. Nothing but boxes and old gardening tools were down here, nothing he could use, until he saw the gap in the wall on the far side.

Giggling wildly, he headed over tearing off his clothes as he did so. Once naked, his cock throbbed like a pulsing heart, cum already seeping from the tip like a leaky tap. The hole in the crumbling wall was just big enough. He gripped his cock and forced it in, ignoring the rough cement and brick that scraped along the edges like sandpaper. For several minutes he fucked the hole in the wall, his cock bleeding from the rough surface, until he roared in ecstasy when he came. He pulled out and already seconds later, he wanted to go again. It could wait, though. He was hungry now.

A few cockroaches darted about on the floor. Davie stepped on them one by one without squashing them then reached down and ate them, chewing slowly to savour the taste. It wasn't enough though. He sat down wondering what else he could eat and if he could really manage to stay down here all night when he remembered what his mother had done to him in the bathroom. Her stupid idea about blocking the devil's entrance. Davie leaned over and pulled out the tampon, now slimy and brown and held it up, letting it swing from side to side as though trying to hypnotise himself. He sniffed it, curious, wondering what a demon's shit smelled like. As bad as anyone else's, he decided. Fuck it, he thought. The things he was going to be doing soon would pale into insignificance compared and really, when one thought about it, it was kinda organic. Davie stuck it in his mouth and swallowed that too. His hunger now satiated, he lay back and tried to get some sleep. Tomorrow was going to be such a fun time had by all. He dreamt that night about fucking his mother on the church's altar while all stood around clapping and cheering, Jesus included.

Chapter 6

When his mother opened the door to the basement the next morning and stuck her head in, at first, she was confused.

"Davie, where are you?"

He watched her step back outside and check the lock. No, he hadn't broken it, although he'd thought about it, just to scare her. Plenty of time for that. She stepped back into the basement, looking around. She grimaced at the sight of splattered bugs, then sniffed and coughed. He'd had a piss near the door when he woke up and it smelled like ammonia. He'd also had a shit and that smelled like heaven. Well, maybe not heaven, more like he'd been eating rotten chicken for a week, saving it all up in his bowels then depositing it later. A welcoming present for Mum.

"Are you hiding in here, Davie? Answer me, you filthy child. I'm taking you to the vicar right now. You're going to confess all your sins and then we're going to see about getting you surgically castrated. Your father has a friend who may be able to do it. You can't live like this, the demons will take you. You'll go to Hell. Davie, where are you?!"

She couldn't see him because he was hanging upside down from the ceiling watching her every move, grinning at her empty threats, naked, his cock already hard and throbbing impatiently. It was time.

"Morning, Mother," he growled.

She gasped and looked up. Then made to scream but before she could do so, Davie jumped down and clamped his lips over hers, shoving his tongue down her throat. She tried to push him off, break free, but those days were over too. He rolled his tongue around her cheeks, her own tongue then pulled away with a loud slurping sound.

"Did you miss me, Mother? I missed you. Look." He took her hand and wrapped her fingers around his cock.

"Davie! Oh, dear Lord, what are you doing? You're possessed. Your eyes, they're bright red, like blood. You're a devil. Back, Satan! Dear God, I beg thee in my time of nee—"

He slapped her across the face.

"God's gone, Mother. Just you and me now. And I'm gonna give you something God never gave you. And I know you want it. You want it haaard, don't you?"

She managed to snatch her hand back, holding it away from her as though she'd just dipped it into something foul and repugnant. Her eyes were bulging, jaw dropped, lost for words. Then she turned and tried to run but Davie had been ready for her. He grabbed her by the hair and brought her back to him, running his tongue across her face like a dog.

"Davie, stop this! Pray with me, Davie. If we pray together, we can stop this foul incarnation inside of you."

"I was thinking more about inside of you, actually. I think you want and need something hard inside you." Still holding her by the hair he dragged her out of the basement and took her upstairs to her bedroom, throwing her on the bed. When she tried to get up and run again, by sheer will of thought she was flung back and her clothes began to tear down the middle, her arms and legs spread wide. He tore the shredded clothes off her, then her bra and knickers leaving her exposed. The

38

thick bush above her pussy was kind of off-putting though so he grabbed a handful and ripped it off. She screamed.

"Tell me you need it," he demanded.

"No, Davie, stop. Listen to me, there's still time. Pray with me, son, and together we'll beat it back into Hell."

"That so? Guess we need a crucifix then, don't we?" He grabbed one that hung above the bed. A wooden one, perhaps three feet long, Jesus sculptured onto it.

"This what we need, Mother? To do some prayin?"

"Y-yes, Davie. Come, pray with me."

"Maybe later."

Jessica was rolled onto her hands and knees, both pinned down by invisible forces.

"If we're gonna pray I guess we need some holy water."

Before she could answer Davie held the crucifix below his cock and pissed up and down the length of the cross. Chuckling, like that of a senile, old man, he gripped the crucifix tightly with one hand while spreading his mother's cheeks and slid the crucifix inside her. Jessica screamed and howled as it slowly filled her, Davie stopping when Jesus' feet reached her like a stopper. He wiggled the cross about and pushed some more until the whole thing was inside her up to the horizontal crossbar, Jesus' head sticking out with that pained, sorrowful look as though feeling embarrassed about his current position. Davie thought it gave a whole new meaning to 'embracing God'.

He stood back to admire his handiwork for a while as he stroked his cock. He thought it would be the ultimate blasphemy if he fucked her while his balls rubbed over Jesus' face back and forth and so he did. He swivelled the cross so Jesus was now upside down and slid himself in, revelling in the tight confines offered by his mother. She was whimpering and groaning now; Davie liked to think it was because she was enjoying it. He told himself she was, despite the tears coursing down her face and the mumbled prayers she was reciting that stung his ears a little. She could pray all she liked; this wasn't like the movies where a few words were going to hurt him.

He pumped back and forth inside her, wiggling the crucifix at the same time, the bedsprings complaining vehemently.

"Keep prayin', Mum. God is with you, Jesus is inside you, listening to your words of prayer. He says it's a little hot in there, though, like Hell."

"Please, Davie, it's me, your mother. I'm sorry for everything. I just wanted you to grow up to be sane and respectful of God. Not like this. Please, stop!"

He thrust harder cutting off her words. She should have thought about that before locking him in the basement, leaving him terrified of the bugs, pissing himself as a small child while hungry and thirsty. Being made to stand outside school reciting passages from the bible in his hand-me-down clothes while all the other kids laughed and threw things at him. Having to stand in front of everyone in church and confess to jerking off—his neighbours, friends' parents, the vicar—while promising he wouldn't do it again and telling them what a filthy boy he was.

Well, look now who the filthy slut was with Jesus shoved up her arse, her son's cock in her pussy while she prayed. Prayed for what? More? Obviously. He rammed her harder and faster, feeling the climax approach. When on the precipice of ejaculation, he pulled his cock out, spun her around and rammed it down her throat. He came with such force, his cock jerking so hard in her mouth he was pretty sure he dislocated her bottom jaw. Cum bubbles formed at her nostrils and popped then ran down her chin like snot.

He removed his cock and glared at the pitiful sight of his mother's gagging and sobbing. But he wasn't finished yet. Far from it. In fact, his cock was already stiffening. Maybe later he'd give her another go. Instead, he slowly pulled out the crucifix and shoved it into her sticky, broken mouth.

"There you go, Mother. Jesus loves ya."

She spat it out and vomited on the bedsheet. "Filthy creature of hell, you are no son of mine. God will cast you back down to the foul pits where you belong. Snake. Serpent. He defeated you once, He will do it again. Vermin. Sick thing, you. Hear me God, take me, show this foul monster who the real Lord is. Show this vile snake who is the righteous one. Make him g—"

Davie picked up the crucifix, covered in her slime and shit and smashed her over the head with it, the crucifix snapping in half. She grunted and continued spewing out her religious crap and by now Davie was bored with it. Picking up the bottom part of the cross with its splintered edges he skewered it into her throat, a great gush of arterial spray shooting up onto his face and in his mouth. He pulled it out and repeated the act, this time so hard it came out the other side. Rapidly, the bed turned crimson as Jessica gargled, Jesus' feet now sticking out of her neck, Jesus' head lodged in her throat. This gave him an idea.

He removed the broken piece of wood, threw it away then clutched her head with both hands and twisted, like trying to pull off the top to a particularly resistant bottle. Muscle and flesh cracked and split open, the sound like tearing off a chicken leg, as yet more blood flowed from the multiple wounds. Her head was twisted almost a hundred and eighty degrees, her dead eyes looking at her spine, yet still it wouldn't come free. There was a pop as her spine column snapped, more flesh splitting open and then in one gargantuan heave, her head burst free from her body, the sound like a bottle of champagne being opened.

"Well, that was harder than I thought," he muttered. He held up his mother's head and admired it as though admiring a trophy he'd just won. "I don't hear you prayin' now, Mother. Is God with you now? Waiting for you at the pearly gates?" Maybe she was downstairs, instead, waiting for him, but he had no intentions of returning anytime soon—he was having far too much fun up here.

Her bottom jaw was indeed broken giving her the appearance of wearing a permanent sneer. Her bloodshot eyes still looked at him accusingly, though, even in death. The bitch. He stuck a finger into each socket and scooped out her eyeballs, then sucked on each one like a hardboiled sweet. He bit down and a mass of jellied puss and goo exploded in his mouth before swallowing. He wondered if eyeballs contained a lot of protein. Didn't testicles contain lots of protein? He thought he'd read somewhere they did. Shame she didn't have any. It was important to keep healthy if one wanted to live a long time. Even though he lived an eternity.

Talking of keeping healthy, he was horny again now, so stuck his raging hard-on into her mouth and fucked her dead throat. When he came, it shot out the other end. That was quite funny, he thought. And now he was hungry.

He kicked the head over into a corner, like a football, then dragged the dead weight downstairs into the basement, leaving behind him a long trail of blood. That would need cleaning before his father came home that evening. His dad always complained if the house was untidy. Might have to change the bedsheets too, he realised. He had plans for his father, but they could wait. No point rushing things. Where was the excitement in that?

The spiders and cockroaches scattered in all directions, but they need not fear for their lives anymore; he had more than enough to keep him occupied. At some point during her decapitation, she had managed to shit herself. He'd read somewhere this was normal during death, so he didn't worry too much about it. It was a shame because his original thoughts had been to start there, but instead, he grabbed her legs and dragged her body towards him. When he'd been with his friends at school, they had always considered the phrase 'eating pussy' to be extremely hilarious. Like, who came up with that? Because as far as they were aware, one didn't actually eat anything, just kinda lick or something. That was what they did in the porn scenes they'd seen, anyway. Now, though, he was going to put real meaning into the phrase.

Having already pulled out most of her bush, he clamped his jaws onto her soggy, wet pussy and crunched down. His teeth, now more like canines thanks to his transformation, easily tore off a great chunk which he greedily chewed and swallowed. It tasted fishy which he guessed could be a combination of sweat, his own cum, and her having pissed herself, which was also a shame. He'd been looking forward to seeing what untainted pussy tasted like. In the flesh, so to speak.

Now that there was a large hole there, and still feeling hungry, he shoved his arm inside her and groped around for something, anything to finish his meal with. Dessert. His fingers wrapped around something soft and squidgy so he tugged until it came loose and pulled it out. He wasn't entirely sure what it was—a liver, kidney, intestine, who knew?—and took a bite. It looked and tasted like a large, rubber sausage; squishy, bloody and hard to chew. Maybe it was her bladder. That would explain the explosion of liquid in his mouth as he bit in half. But hadn't she pissed herself when dying? That was weird. He wondered what her bowels would taste like now they were empty. That was for later, though. Now, after having an early lunch he was feeling drowsy and he still had the bedroom and that bloody trail to take care of before his dad came home. Never-ending, that was what it felt like. Who ever said being a demon was easy?

Chapter 7

Mike parked his car and sat staring at his semi-detached home before going in. He wondered what stresses and toils his wife had been through today that he would undoubtedly have to listen to for the next two hours before she even considered asking him how his day had been.

Then, there would follow the inevitable psalm reading, which was fine with him, but he did think she got a little caried away with things sometimes. Yes, God may be watching over them, but did He really listen or care too much about them? It didn't always seem that way. And one of the things that caused him to blaspheme and question everything in private was that damn son of theirs, Davie. It was as if he tried to push them, especially his mother, on purpose, as if it was some kind of a game. Davie knew damn well that profanity was not allowed in the house and yet a few times he had been heard to say the word 'shit' in his bedroom and even the dreaded F word. Jessica had nearly had a heart attack. And then nearly beat Davie to death.

And yet, even though he would never dare question her decisions, or go against her, he had to admit that punishing the teenage boy for masturbating was wrong. He'd tried to argue with her but she wouldn't have it. It was perfectly normal in young boys, he tried to tell her. All boys and girls did things when going through puberty, but no, she wouldn't have it. If it had been up to her she would have taken Davie to a surgeon and had him surgically castrated. She was still talking about doing so.

He tried to tell himself for the umpteenth time that her heart was in the right place and she just wanted the best for their son but damn she could be so maddening and over the top with her religious beliefs. To the point it made him wonder why she had wanted to get married in the first place, let alone have a child. He hadn't seen her naked since that day, nearly sixteen years ago, and really, there were only so many times one could lock oneself in the toilet and glare at videos while relieving oneself. Good job his secretary was so understanding. If Jessica ever discovered his cardinal sins, he would be joining Davie at the castrator's chair.

Mike took a deep breath, shook his head at his relative bad fortune, and stepped out of the car. He shouldn't complain, he told himself. Others had it worse. And she was a damn good cook, he had to give her that. If only she didn't have this silly aversion to pork. As a kid, pork sausages had been Mike's favourite; now, if he wanted pork he had to go to a bar and order it. Maybe he'd have another word with her over dinner. Nothing like a big, juicy sausage washed down with a nice glass of red.

He opened the front door, tentatively, expecting perhaps another shouting match between mother and son but tonight it was surprisingly and pleasantly quiet. He couldn't smell any cooking coming from the kitchen, though, which was slightly disturbing. Wouldn't be the first time she'd forgotten to cook lunch while having a marathon session with her trusty bible. And Mike was damn hungry, right now. His secretary had exhausted him this time around.

"Honey! I'm home!" he called.

No answer.

46

"Jessica? Davie? Anyone home?"

Could she have followed through with her threat and taken Davie first to the local vicar and then to see his colleague about castrating Davie? Surely not. Not without telling him first.

He headed to the kitchen and was dismayed to see there was nothing cooked, nothing prepared. No one was in the living room and it was deathly quiet in here—something that unfortunately was extremely rare to encounter. He headed upstairs, all the time calling out to his wife and son. He checked Davie's room—he wasn't in there. Then he went to his bedroom and peered in. He frowned. Something was wrong.

The bed was unmade, that was the first sign. Never, ever would Jessica dream of not making the bed as soon as she got up in the mornings. It was one of her many obsessions, saying that anyone who didn't make the bed first thing in the morning was uncouth and sinful. Now, there were no sheets, no blankets, no pillows as if she was preparing to throw the thing out. He stepped inside and realised something else was amiss, although he couldn't quite put his finger on what. Something minor, perhaps, but in this household would equate to something massive. And then, when he caught the whiff of something odd, he realised. The window was closed. Jessica left the window open all day regardless of whether it was freezing or raining. To clear out the impure thoughts, she said. She did the same with Davie which drove him mad.

He looked to the carpet and that was when he saw the stain. There was a trail that looked like someone had walked around the room then left with an open bottle of red wine, its contents spilling onto their nice carpet.

Oh no, what on earth have these two been getting up to now? he asked himself. Had they had another epic fight, Jessica perhaps trying to drag the boy to see the local priest and he had refused? Had then grabbed a bottle of wine and threatened her with it? Wouldn't be the first time, either. Whatever had happened, it was serious. He could only assume Jessica had finally managed to overcome their son and take him somewhere. That or she had locked him in the basement again.

Now panicking slightly, he rushed downstairs to the basement. The door was open which he hadn't noticed until now and when he peered down into the gloomy, dark room, it smelled disgusting. A rich, coppery smell mixed with something like ammonia and a stench reminiscent of the sewers on a hot day. He didn't really want to go down there now that he was here.

"Davie, are you there?"

He strained to listen and was pretty sure he could hear something. Heavy breathing, perhaps, or…slurping was it? Almost like a dog slavering, just as his mother's used to do when eating.

"Davie? Where's your mother?"

He thought of hitting the light switch but he wasn't so sure he really wanted to do that, either. The shock could be profound.

"Davie, I know you're down there. Where is your mother?"

The slurping/slavering sound stopped. Replaced by a shuffling and then Mike gasped when two bright red orbs appeared, looking up at him. They were eyes, he knew that immediately. And he thought he knew who

48

they belonged to. He recalled that long stain on the bedroom floor and knew what that had really been as well. Slowly, he backed away as those twin orbs came ever closer, and he slammed the door shut, locking it as he did so. He needed to call the police. Jessica had finally gone too far and had pushed Davie into doing something despicable. But wait, no. Not the police, they couldn't help Davie now. Mike wasn't close to being as religious as his wife but he knew enough to know what those burning, red eyes meant.

So he did the only logical thing he could think of.

###

Reverend Wilson arrived within the hour. He had been shocked when Mike told him what he suspected. To the point he assumed it was some kind of morbid joke, but knowing this family, especially his wife, Jessica, jokes of such a nature would be considered blasphemous. And then there was Jessica herself. What Mike had insinuated was terrible and evil. He knew that there had been issues with Davie but to imply this…God would never allow it.

He knocked on the door and waited both impatiently and nervously. Nervous because the way Mike had been practically screaming at him on the phone suggested something had happened. Something bad. The door finally opened and Mike greeted him with wild, terrified eyes, grabbing him by the arm and dragging him in.

"Oh, thank God, you came. I didn't think you would. I thought of phoning the police but they can't help us in these matters, only God. You have to do something. An exorcism, I dunno, because I ca—"

"Wait, wait, wait, slow down. An *exorcism*?"

"Yes! Because my boy, he's not a boy anymore, he's a devil. Satan's spawn. You should have seen his eyes. Bright red, like lasers. So terrible. Do something before he kills us all. He's already killed my wife I'm sure of it."

"Where is he now?" he asked slowly. This man was surely delusional. He might be a man of the cloth but the idea of demons and monsters was not something he necessarily believed in.

"He's in the basement, I locked him in down there."

"And you haven't seen or heard from Jessica?"

"No. She doesn't have a mobile phone, she's against them, but I know that's her blood on the bedroom floor."

Maybe Mike wasn't as delusional as he first believed him to be. "Okay, let me see the boy."

"Right but be careful. He's dangerous. A demon from Hell."

"I shall be the judge of that."

Mike led him to the basement door under the stairs and unlocked the padlock. As soon as the door opened the slightest amount so Mike could check Davie wasn't standing directly behind it, the smell hit Reverend Wilson. He gagged and covered his mouth, his eyes watering. It was the most disgusting thing he had ever smelled in his life. During the war he had served in the trenches and the stench of rotting, decomposing men had been terrible. That, combined with the foul odour of human faeces where terrified soldiers had literally messed themselves was something he never forgot. Down there in that basement exactly the same stench was wafting up to greet him like a bad memory.

"Dear Lord," he spluttered, wiping his eyes with a

handkerchief.

"Yes, I know. Terrible, isn't it?" Mike opened the door wider and peered in. "Look for yourself, he's down there."

Reverend Wilson hadn't come prepared for meeting demons, but he did carry with him his trusty crucifix that he wore on a chain around his neck. He took it off and gripped it firmly in his hand before stepping into the basement. To his left he saw the light switch. He made to turn it on but a dreadful, howling shriek almost caused him to fall down the basement steps.

"Fucking leave it off!" said the foul voice.

Reverend Wilson did as he was told. Surely that wasn't Davie down there that just said that? It didn't sound like a human was capable of making such a noise. Then there came a tearing sound, followed by slavering. A long, loud fart echoed around the basement then chuckling.

"I told you," whispered Mike.

Part of Reverend Wilson wanted to find out exactly what had become of this boy, another just wanted to get the hell out. It did indeed sound like something had possessed the boy, but demons didn't exist. Did they?

He took another step forward then abruptly stopped. It was pitch black down there but suddenly two bright red orbs glared up at him, blinking rapidly. A growl reverberated around the room.

"Hello, Reverend. Nice to meet you. How are the choir boys back at the church? They suck your cock good, did they? You like the blonde one best, don't you. What's his name? Mickey. Rub your hands through his curly mop while he sucks your dick. Does your wife, Alison, know about this? Have you told her,

Reverend?"

"Lies! Blasphemer." He held up his crucifix, but his hands were shaking badly. Not necessarily because the thing down there was scaring him but because what it had said was true.

The creature that might or might not have been Davie chuckled again. "How about those nice, firm buttocks of little Gary? Like to grip them nice and hard when you're slippin' into him, Reverend?"

"You be quiet, foul beast! Father of lies! Your words mean nothing!"

"Hahaha. Oh, I think they do. Tasty, tasty Gary. The poor boy sobbing as you fuck him. No help from God with Gary is there, Reverend?"

"I've had enough of this, you disgusting, foul thing."

He made to leave when something landed at his foot. He was about to pick it up when he realised what it was. A bone. Picked clean it looked disturbingly similar to a thigh bone. Then something else landed beside it. Reverend Wilson gasped and whimpered when he saw the fleshy mound and the woman's nipple sitting proudly in the centre. He slammed the door shut and locked it again.

"Mike, whatever you do don't listen to it. It is the master of lies. I'm going to speak to the bishop immediately. You were right; we need an exorcist here as soon as possible."

"What about my wife? Is she down there with him?"

To that, Reverend Wilson did not know what to say.

Chapter 8

Davie hadn't laughed so much in a very long time. He didn't need to see the Reverend's face to know he had seriously freaked the dirty, fucking pervert out. Such a bad name God's disciples were creating for themselves and there was a reason for it. They were all fucking little boys or having their cocks sucked by them while preaching His name. If God truly was watching over them, they would all be serving his master instead of the other, false God. It made everything a mockery. Father of lies? They were the ones preaching lies and deceit, not him. And they knew it.

It was his job to teach them that as well. Make them understand they were all better off following his master rather than the fake one. Starting with this exorcist if and when he turned up. They were fun to play with and he was going to make this the funniest game he had ever played in his life. But first to deal with his father. Wouldn't do to have the man running down the streets screaming before his fun was over. He was strong and powerful but it only took one who, if aware of the right words to say, could banish him back to where he came from. And that couldn't happen.

He could hear his father upstairs pacing around the house, no doubt terrified and worried, as he should be. Davie tore off the left cheek of his mother and chewed absently, while considering what he should do to his father. Something fitting with the puny man's character, he thought. The weakling. The man with no balls. Not daring to speak up for himself, having to fuck his secretary in secret because his own wife wouldn't

53

give him any. Pathetic. Everyone should fuck at least five times a day, that was his motto. Didn't matter with who or what, no need to be picky. If there was any sin in the world, it was that there wasn't enough fucking going around. He'd taunted the priest about it, but privately he was proud of the man. If he returned, he could perhaps take his soul as well, use him to converts the infidels.

Davie finished off eating his mother's cheek, swallowed it and pulled himself to his feet. The cockroaches—his friends, now—scattered. He looked down at what remained of his mother—not a lot. She hadn't been a large woman but it was still amazing how much meat she had on her. Enough to feed the five thousand. Her organs and intestines now showed through the large hole in her stomach, some hanging out from where he'd pulled lumps off. Those were the tastiest—warm and soft. No fat or bone or gristle to chew through either. Which was why he was saving them for later. Actually, thinking about that, he pulled out her long intestine and hung it around his neck like a string of sausages. Something to chew on later in case he got peckish.

He headed up the stairs and the door was blown from its hinges, crashing against the far wall. His dad would know by now he was free and unless he jumped out the top floor window there was no escape for him. Davie headed upstairs looking for him, whistling some senseless tune as he did so.

He found his father cowering in the corner of his bedroom.

"Hi, Dad. Watcha doin'?"

"Get away from me, Devil's spawn. Thing of evil.

Don't come any closer or I'll—"

"What, Dad? What will you do? Spank me, lock me in the basement? Make me recite shit from the bible? We could do that together. Pray for Mum, whadaya say?"

"Back, Satan," he said and held up a cross as though trying to ward off a vampire.

Davie snatched it off him and threw it away. "That won't do you any good. Didn't do mum any good either. I decided to bring a keepsake with me, like in memory of her? What do you think, Dad?" He held out the foul-smelling intestine like an offering. "So we never forget her." Then he took a bite out of it and spat it at his father. It landed on his cheek and slithered down like a bogey. Mike whimpered.

Mike tried to make a run for it.

He stopped before he even made it out the door, his back arched, body frozen as though time had stopped. Then, as if invisible hands had reached out for him, he was thrown back onto the bed.

"Going somewhere, Dad?"

The man looked like he was suffering an epileptic fit, violent spasms rocking his body, muscles and veins taut and stretched. He foamed at the mouth as though rabid.

"Okay, stop." Instantly, his father ceased spasming. He looked like he'd been on the verge of a heart attack and that couldn't happen. That was the easy way out.

"Get up."

Mike did as he was told, as though he'd been hypnotised. He was crying now too, like a baby.

"Please, I'm your father, don't hurt me. Just go."

Davie sighed. Pathetic.

"Let's go."

He grabbed his father by the arm and led him back downstairs then to the basement, throwing him down the steps. Davie turned on the light. His father took in a great lungful of air and screamed.

"C'mon, it's not that bad," said Davie impatiently. Well, maybe it was a bit. Mike's wife lay sprawled on her back or rather what was left of her. A great hole like the entrance to a cave sat where her stomach should be revealing the organs and intestines Davie hadn't eaten yet. Her breasts had both been torn off leaving fleshy, rotting wounds, one of the breasts still lying at the top of the stairs from where he'd thrown it at the Reverend. Where her eyes should have been were now empty sockets like craters filled with sticky, drying blood. Her eyeballs had tasted pretty good, Davie had to admit. And what was left of her face, which wasn't a lot, looked as though some savage dog had had a tug-of-war with another, tearing and ripping the flesh off, leaving mainly her skull showing. One of her arms was missing which Davie had gnawed upon last night, the bone also up with the fleshy breast. So yeah, Davie had to admit, it probably did look a little gruesome. To the untrained eye.

"Breakfast's ready, Dad. Get stuck in."

Mike tried to crawl away, the strength evidently having left him.

"You're not going anywhere until you've eaten your breakfast. That's what you and mum were always saying to me, so practice what you preach, right? If you don't eat your breakfast, I'll make you eat it. And then it will be me deciding which part you actually get. Does that sound fair? I think it does."

"Please, just go away. You've done enough as it is. And it wasn't me that locked you in the basement, was it? I didn't make you stand there in church and tell everyone your secrets, did I?"

"You didn't fucking stop her either, you coward. You're pathetic, you wouldn't even serve me in Hell as a slave, so fucking eat."

"No, I refuse. The exorcist will be here shortly. He'll send you back to where you belong." He started reciting some prayer which only infuriated Davie more. It was poison to his ears.

"All right, don't say I didn't warn you."

Davie hovered inches off the floor, as though levitating, then floated over to his father. He lowered and grabbed him around the throat then threw him onto the already-rotting remains of his wife. Mike shrieked and tried to push himself off her but Davie had him gripped firmly.

"Eat!"

"No! I won't! You can't make me!"

"For fuck's sake. The things one has to do."

First, he rammed his father's head into the fleshy mess that used to be her breast, now filling with maggots and flies laying eggs. Mike vomited making the situation much worse for himself. Jessica's tongue was now a swollen, bloated thing, black and looking like it was about to explode at any second. Davie pulled it out and held it up, letting it swing back and forth as though he'd just squashed a large bug. Then, he lifted Mike's head, and with vomit now on his face, shoved the tongue down his throat and covered his mouth with his hand. Mike's face turned red, green, white, which Davie thought was pretty amazing, his cheeks puffing out as he gagged but eventually was forced to swallow it.

"See, wasn't so bad, was it? She always did have a poisonous tongue on her, didn't she? Bit like her pussy. Man, you don't want to know what *that* tasted like!"

Mike was panting heavily, tears streaming down his face. Davie couldn't tell if he was trying to puke or avoid doing so.

"Bad heart too, I reckon. Black and poisonous as well. Shall we find out?"

He reached in, fumbling about for a while through the woman's ribcage until he found it. He wrapped his hand around what he assumed to be her heart and pulled. It came away with a resounding plopping sound. It wasn't black as he predicted but it did look like some poisonous, foul thing. He held it out for his dad to eat.

"No, I won't. Go back to hell where you belong, you serpent of Satan."

Davie sighed. He gripped his father's throat and squeezed the sides of his mouth with his fingers. The brute force caused Mike's mouth to finally open. He pushed the heart inside and forced his mouth closed again.

"I'd chew on it for a bit first, if I were you. You might choke."

He kept his hand clamped over Mike's mouth so he couldn't spit it out. Eventually, seeing that he had no choice, he began to chew. It took a while but he finally ate it all.

"See?! Now she's a part of you forever. Gives a whole new meaning to the phrase 'love you to bits', doesn't it?"

Mike said nothing, his face pallid, glaring at Davie

as though he might try and kill him. Which wasn't going to happen.

"Right, that's breakfast done. Better get this over with, I suppose."

Davie stood up and, using his mind, made his father rise of his own accord as well until he hovered in the air, arms outstretched as though being crucified. The man started choking, face turning bright red. Davie tore off his trousers and underwear so he hung there in all his glory, his limp dick tiny and shrivelled. As his throat was slowly squeezed, not enough to kill him, just enough so he was aware, piss and shit ran down his legs, splattering on the floor.

"Where's God now, Dad? I don't see him coming to help, do you?"

Mike spluttered and groaned as he tried to say something, yet this was impossible as his Adam's apple was being crushed. Davie grabbed his dick and tugged. He kept doing so until it was ripped from his body, then with his fingernails like claws, slashed his sack open, so the contents joined the rest of his bodily waste dribbling down his legs. These he rammed into Mike's mouth as well. With his throat constricted this time he couldn't swallow them so they sat there dangling like obscene tumours.

"Seeing God yet, Dad? Bright lights at the end of a tunnel? The Nazarene waiting with open arms? Angels flutterin' overhead waiting to take you away? Whadaya see, Dad? How about Hell? You see that? 'cause that's where you're going."

Davie sunk both his hands into his father's stomach and ripped it open, as though opening a gift. It was like opening the gates to a dam. Liquid and stomach acids spilled onto the floor as he opened his chest, like opening a book in the middle, revealing everything. His heart still beat feebly behind his ribcage, Mike barely alive, feeling everything. Davie started tearing out each individual organ, throwing them away like discarded junk until only his ribcage remained. He left his heart until last, pulling it out, taking a bite, then letting his father drop to the floor. Still not quite finished, and knowing the exorcist shouldn't take much longer, he took Mike's head in his hands and twisted just as he did with his mother. It came away with a resounding crunching sound as the spinal cord snapped. Then, picking up his mother's head as well, he carried them both upstairs to the living room, sitting them proudly on the mantelpiece. His father's dick, still in his mouth, he removed and put inside his mother's. There, if that didn't scare off the exorcist, nothing would.

Chapter 9

"You have to come immediately, Terence. It was horrific. Never in all my days as a priest have I ever seen or heard of anything so...so evil and corrupt. It must be banished," said Reverend Wilson.

He had run from that house, stopping only to vomit in the Simpson's garden, then nearly having a heart attack from both the shock and exertion of running. What that boy—that thing—had done, had become, was nothing less than abomination. Something that had no place on God's earth. Something that should have remained in the corrupted lands of Hell, never to be released. The smell, those eyes, the things it said, the way it spoke, it was an evil thing that needed to die.

And poor Jessica, the innocent, helpless victim in all this, that had never done wrong to anyone. The woman who only tried to be good and do good, praising the Lord's name, spreading His good name, not a shred of nastiness in her. All she had wanted to do was raise her son the correct way so he came to learn and understand respect and what had he done? How had he repaid her? By turning into a...a...

He couldn't even say the word. Forty-five years in the priesthood and preaching about good and evil, God and Satan, but he hadn't really believed all that. Demons were metaphors for all the bad in the world carried out by humans. They didn't actually exist, with long, pointy tails, and horns on their heads, scurrying up walls and spouting filth.

Well, you were wrong about that, weren't you?

He could still see that...woman's thing staring up at him like an eyeball. And now, here he was begging the only man he knew with the capabilities to perform an exorcism to go there immediately and he was making excuses.

"I need proof, Harry. I need permission from the Bishop. You don't just walk into somebody's home and do an exorcism. There's procedure. Especially when it involves a minor."

"But you didn't see him! It's not a minor anymore. It's not even human. It threw…pieces of Jessica at me. Just come and look, see for yourself. The husband, Mike, is in grave danger. If you don't do something right now, and something happens to him, it will be on your hands."

"Don't you go threatening me, Harry. I don't make the rules. If something was to go wrong or—"

"Just come! Please! Take a look for yourself. You'll see when you go in that Godforsaken place that the boy has been possessed. You won't have to do anything. Just the sight of him will be enough. And the smell, of course."

Terence stared at Harry for some time, no doubt contemplating whether to heed to the man's seemingly mad demands or not. Harry stared back, hoping he looked as terrified as he felt. If not, the man would insist on going through the motions, and that could take days.

"Okay," he said after what sounded like an eternity, "I'll come. But I'm not promising anything. I'm just going to assess the situation and I will decide after that."

"Oh, thank you!"

"But you're coming with me."

The fuck I am.

###

They arrived shortly afterwards. They would have arrived much earlier had Terence not had to spend almost an hour telling Harry that if he didn't accompany him then *he* wouldn't be going either. Harry had looked on the verge of tears such was his terror at having to return to the house. Terence reminded him that he was a man of faith and therefore should use that faith to remain strong. Harry had countered that when it came to demons, unless God Himself flew down to help out, faith had very little to do with it. The kid had torn off Jessica's breast, for God's sake! Terence wondered if old Harry wasn't over-reacting a little.

Eventually, Terence convinced him that if the kid was as badly possessed as he was suggesting they wouldn't be remaining in the house for very long anyway, so reluctantly Harry agreed. And now they were standing at the gate looking up at the windows for any sign of the boy or his father and Harry a blabbering mess refusing to go any further.

"You don't need me to go any further. Go knock on the door and if no one answers just go inside. I'll wait here."

"I can't just walk into a stranger's home unannounced. You know them, I don't. The man of the house might think I'm a thief or something."

"The thing that used to be his son killed and mutilated the man's wife. I hardly think he'll be too concerned about burglars right now. He might…he might not even be alive. He could be lying there somewhere in great agony. I'll wait here and if I hear you shout or scream or something then I can run and call the police."

Damn this coward.

Terence headed down the garden path alone. He made to knock on the door then saw it was slightly ajar. He pushed it open and tensed, ready for the worst. Maybe there were burglars or something inside. The first thing to hit him was the smell. He brought out his handkerchief and covered his nostrils. It smelled as though squatters had been staying here and hadn't bothered using the toilet; instead, choosing to do their business in whatever corner they could find.

"Hello? Is anybody home? Mr. Simpson?"

No answer came which made Terence nervous. Maybe Harry hadn't been exaggerating, after all. From what the man said, the Simpsons were upstanding, respected neighbours; their home shouldn't be smelling like this. He turned around to see Harry standing at the gate. He shrugged his shoulders. *Anything? You see anything?* Terence was going to tell him to come see for himself but refrained. Maybe it wasn't such a bad idea that he remained at the gate. Terence was beginning to feel very uncomfortable. He pulled out the gold crucifix he always carried in his pocket and gripped it tightly, then stepped inside, murmuring the Lord's prayer as he did so.

Harry had mentioned the boy had been down in the basement. The door was wide open and an even greater stench emanating from down there. He took a tentative step closer and peered inside. It was pitch black and silent. Terence had performed numerous exorcisms before but had never had to do one on his own, always accompanied by a fellow priest or a doctor as the law required. He really did not want to go into that basement on his own.

"Hello?" he called, his voice echoing back at him.

No answer.

Okay, we'll come back to that.

He moved instead to the living room, noticing a slimy trail on the floor which made him even more concerned.

"Hello? Anyone home? Mr. Simpson? Davie?"

He was about to turn and head upstairs when he happened to glance at the mantelpiece. Yes, Mr and Mrs Simpson were indeed home, but not in the manner in which he had hoped and expected to find them. His initial reaction had been that he was looking at some kind of weird ornament or sculpture, something from one of those cheap Chinese shops. He then had to mentally recall which month this was because what he was looking at also suggested it was Halloween.

But it wasn't.

The heads of who he presumed to be the parents sat there, what little flesh remained now swarmed over by maggots, flies crawling and buzzing in and around the various holes in their faces. Their eyes were missing, sockets filled with some rusty-coloured liquid that might once have been blood. Most of the flesh had been eaten away it seemed, bits dangling like confetti at a party. Inside the woman's mouth sat something, Terence wasn't quite sure what. Wanting to run from this house immediately and call the police, yet also needing to know what he was truly dealing with, he took a step closer. His suspicions were confirmed. Sitting in the woman's mouth was a flaccid little penis, that seemed to be throbbing even in death until he realised they were small bugs and maggots squirming in there, using the tip of his penis as their entry point.

Terence cried out in horror and turned to run.

"Hello, priest. Going somewhere?"

###

Davie had heard the two men arrive long beforehand and remembered the priest from before. The other had more of an ominous, more powerful aura about him which had initially troubled him, but then he remembered who he was and that the chances of this shaman actually knowing the words to hurt him were slim. He was going to have lots of fun with this one. *Let's test your faith, Mr Preacher.*

"You, you treacherous snake. Lord of all vermin. God, I call upon thee to cast out this demon, banish this creature from your lands and send it back from whence it came."

He held up his cross as he spoke which made no difference to Davie. The man's eyes reeked of fear and horror. Davie guessed he didn't look a pretty sight. When he'd glanced in the mirror earlier, bits of his parent's flesh were stuck to his cheeks and face like a toddler eating with bare hands, cramming food in. Blood was smeared everywhere, covering the clothes he'd been wearing for some time, and he still hadn't figured a way to stop shitting himself which was now becoming quite uncomfortable; the heavy weight sloshing about and up his back every time he sat down. The boy was long gone by now, his presence too distant to use his mind and figure a way to stop it from happening. The thing preventing the exorcist from escaping was now no more human than the boy's parents were alive.

The demon took the cross from the exorcist's hand,

whipped out his dick, pissed on the cross, then stuck it in his mouth, sucking on it.

"Holy water, priest. Mmm, love it! Want some?"

"Foul beast from Hell. You don't scare me. God, I ask of thee—"

"For fuck's sake. Your God isn't coming to help you, priest. No one is coming to help you. Only me. I'm going to help you understand who the true God is."

With a flick of his wrist, he sent the exorcist flying across the room, to crash against the far wall and slide down. Time to get to work. He ripped off his now-tattered clothes until he was naked, the heavy lump that had been kept in place in his trousers now running down his legs like a mudslide. That was better. Smelled pretty good too, he had to admit. Who would have thought human flesh could produce such a wonderful aroma?

The exorcist tried to pull himself to his feet as he saw his intentions, his cock throbbing in eager anticipation, cum already dripping from the tip. He reached Terence and pulled him to his feet.

"Your God says that on the seventh day He rested but that's a lie. You wanna know what He did? He fucked all his angels. Took out His great, hairy cock and fucked them all up the arse. I know, I was there. Fucked me too. One great, big orgy. That's how rain was created, did you know? All that cum raining down on the world. Who would have thought? That's why His son's girlfriend was a prostitute. And let me tell you, she was one dirty, little slut. Took it anywhere and everywhere. Fucked her myself."

"Father of Lies, I command thee to return to your foul world. Your words mean nothing."

"Command? I command you to get undressed."

Asmodeus gripped him around the throat and with his other hand tore off the man's clothes. He gripped his shrivelled cock in his hand and squeezed. To Terence's horror, it began to harden.

"Hehe, see, Terence? Who's lying now? Sex is universal, doesn't differentiate between good and bad, right and wrong. Even you lot with your vows and celibacy still can't resist. Ask Harry waiting outside. He sure didn't let his choir boys resist. Made sure they sucked it good and proper. Like you're going to do. But, and I guess we should be true to ourselves and those we worship, if your man Jesus suffered before dying, I guess you should do the same. He took the whip and the spear, what are you willing to take? My spear up your arse?"

"I fear you not, serpent. God is watching over me, He will see fit to spare me."

"That so? I suppose we better find out if that's the case, then."

He could smell the fear coming off Terence in waves. It might have been his bowels as well, it was hard to determine. With fingernails like talons, Asmodeus raked them in strategic places up and down the exorcist's body taking special care around his balls and cock, still firmly gripped in his other hand.

"Jesus paid for his sins naked, Terence, and so shall you."

And with that, the blood beginning to ooze from the gashes like water from a cracked vase, he started peeling. He took a handful from Terence's neck and pulled. It was like peeling off old wallpaper. Terence screamed, his body shaking in agony as the skin was torn from his body. It came off easier than the demon had expected. First, a large flap from his chest down to his cock, exposing the muscle and sinewy tissue, then he turned the man around and pulled off the skin covering his back. From a distance, with his red chest and back, arms, legs and face still creamy white, he might have looked like a tourist who has fallen asleep at the beach all day, now severely sunburnt.

Terence howled and screamed, his bowels and bladder gushing their contents everywhere. Asmodeus let go of him now, the man in too much shock to even attempt to run. He took his arm, peeled of the skin down to his fingers then ripped it all off in one go, repeating the action with his other arm. Next, he did the same to his legs. All that remained of anything resembling skin was his face and groin. He did the face first, leaving nothing except a mop of bloody, grey hair on top.

"Okay, this bit might sting a little," he said, then performed an impromptu circumcision on the man, peeling back the skin as though pulling off a condom. He'd always wondered what it looked like behind that thick layer, now he knew.

"There you go, shaman. As naked as Jesus was on the cross. But, and here's the thing, it didn't stop there. Oh no, it got worse, far worse."

He dragged Terence to his feet, his fingers now sinking into the soft muscle tissue with the protective layer of skin and turned him around. He bent him over the back of the sofa, a red raw arsehole coated in streaks of brown and slowly pushed his throbbing cock inside revelling in the warmth and tightness.

"They fucked him hard, Terence, I'm sorry to say.

69

All of them did, in fact. His wife watched them do it. I think she fucked them afterwards as well, can't remember now. Must have gotten pretty horny watching it all."

Terence was incapable of responding, only managing to articulate a few groans. Gripping his fleshy, sticky body was a whole new experience. It was like fucking someone who has been covered in honey or trying to fuck a sex doll made of jelly. Then he had another idea.

He pulled out, a slurping sound accompanying like a fart. Using the power of his mind he made Terence rise into the air upside down, his arms outstretched, an upside-down crucifix. He forced open the almost-dead man's mouth and slipped his cock in while massaging Trence's own cock into hardening, which it did, something Asmodeus found quite amazing. The human body was quite the surprise. It then occurred to him Terence could surprise him yet further by biting down on his cock, especially now that he had no lips. He pulled out, punched the man in the mouth and waited for him to spit his teeth out. That was better. Still not quite the same, though. He lowered the man until his head was touching the floor then entered him from behind again. Much better. Like having his cock wrapped in cotton wool. He continued this way for some time, trying to take as long as possible, enjoy the moment, until he could stand it no longer. He pulled out, went around to Terence's face, squatted, then came in his mouth and eyes.

"Jesus wore a crown of thorns and a mask of blood. This is the best I could do under the circumstances, Terence. Hope it's okay. I mean, you all preach about getting closer to God, understanding His son's pain, so I think it's kinda fitting, don't you?"

Terence merely whimpered and groaned.

"I'll take that as a yes. Now, Jesus was stabbed by a spear as he hung on the cross. I don't happen to have a spear with me, unless we consider my cock to be one, which in a way it is, so we'll have to do the next best thing. Use what's available to us, so to speak, right?"

Asmodeus willed Terence's cock to stiffen again, after temporarily softening then with the tip of his fingernail, now long and sharp like a needle, slowly entered the slit of his cock, pushing it all the way until his finger slipped inside too, a grotesque bulging from the inside out as though some bug was trying to burrow its way in. He finger-fucked him like this for some time then removed it again, the hole in the tip of his cock obscene and huge.

"Now that I imagine is what it was like to be stabbed by that spear you folks so often mention. You all talk about the suffering of Jesus, and what he allowed to happen, well, you can now tell everyone you did the same. Makes you feel closer to God? I don't see Him coming to save you yet, Terence. Wherever could He be?"

He then remembered Reverend Wilson was still outside. He went to the window, opened it and sure enough there he was.

"Hey, Reverend! Terence here is having a wonderful time! He's having so much fun. Asks if you'd like to join him? Do some serious prayin' to God. I call it The Re-enactment. Ball-breaking fun. You comin', 'cause Terence is?"

Harry Wilson shrieked and fled.

The demon chuckled.

He was getting a little peckish now so went and retrieved the cock sitting in his mother's mouth and chewed thoughtfully as he considered his next and final move. And really, it was quite obvious how things should finish. When he was younger, his host's father had apparently fancied himself as a DIY expert from what he could retrieve from the boy's memories, always making stuff in the garage, usually religion-orientated to please his wife, so the garage was well-stocked with tools and materials. He left Terence still dangling upside down and went to hunt what he wanted to finish the lesson. It didn't take long.

"Now then, Terence. Jesus was crucified on the cross. Cruel nails in his wrists and ankles. Poor guy suffered a lot, right, so I think it's only fair we finish today's little lesson respectively. Kinda like a homage. What do you say? I think your name will be spoken about for centuries to come. They'll probably make you a saint. Won't be worth shit when you're with me in Hell, but it's the thought that counts, right?"

Harry Wilson was probably on the phone to the police already by now, so Asmodeus assumed he didn't have a lot of time left. Not that the police would be able to do a lot and they would probably run screaming anyway, but they might always come right back with armed officers and that would totally fuck up his day. So he gripped Terence around the ankle and led him to the nearest wall.

"Right, this is it, exorcist. Just remember what I said. You're doing this for Jesus. Your name will live forever, unlike you unfortunately. I don't suppose you'll last for three days like Jesus did either, which is a shame. So…"

He left Terence hanging against the wall and picked up the hammer and a handful of the six-inch nails he'd brought back with him. One nail went straight into the ankle, cutting through bone like a knife through butter until it was firmly embedded in the wall. Terence groaned, whatever was left in his bowels made an encore appearance and dribbled down his chest. Then Asmodeus did the same to his other ankle, then to both his wrists, leaving him nailed there. He stood back to admire his handiwork then picked up some more nails. One went straight through Terence's eyeball, then the next, making a nice, popping sound. To stop the man shitting himself even in hell, several were pounded into his arsehole, done at an angle so the hole was permanently blocked and as a last and fitting gesture of good will, just before Terence breathed his last, one nail went down the tip of his cock, puncturing the flesh as it popped out the other side and one more nailed his cock to the wall.

"There we go, Terence. All done. I'll see you in Hell."

As a tribute, he turned his parent's heads so it appeared they were spectators at the morbid game. In the distance he could hear police car sirens, so he rammed the hammer down Terence's throat and left to hide in the basement. Once the police saw Jessica's mutilated, dismembered body, parts of her lying around everywhere, he didn't think they would be returning for a while. Not until they'd stopped puking everywhere anyway. More than enough time for him to make an escape and hide up for a while. And he knew just the right place to hide and who to wait for.

Chapter 10

"I'd like to welcome a new parishioner to our church," said Reverend Wilson to his flock. He beckoned the man to rise and salute his fellow church members who were all clapping.

"This is Michael Seudomas. We're very happy to have you with us and we hope you find God's love in your prayers in both the good and bad times, just as we all have."

It was amazing what a haircut and a little fuckery with people's heads could do. Harry had not the slightest idea who he was. None of them did. It had been a week since Terence's gruesome discovery and a nationwide hunt was on the way for Davie Simpson, who hadn't been seen since. This was because he had been hiding in the church itself, down in the basement where nobody ever went. He'd been feeding on dogs and cats that he picked up at night and when he was ready, had presented himself to Reverend Wilson as a new person to the village, a devout Christian he told him who was looking for lots of love. Harry Wilson hadn't battered an eyelid, embracing the new member as if he were their saviour. Well, Michael, as he now called himself to the parishioners, was indeed their saviour and he had lots of love to share with them himself.

"Thank you, Reverend. I have lots of love to give to everyone. It's a part of my nature. Give and receive, that's my motto. Both at the same time if possible too."

This caused a few eyebrows to raise.

"I'm here today to give a lot of love. Just as Terence gave his life to God so that he be remembered by all,

I'd like to do the same today. Give life that is. Maybe a little head as well. I'm sure God would appreciate if we gave Him some head. And just as Jesus gave his life for us on the cross I'd like to return that favour."

"Well, that's, umm, very generous, Michael," said a confused-looking Harry. "And how do you suppose we go about returning that favour?"

"Well, I'm not entirely sure how accurate the report is, and I can't quite remember myself, but I do recall that his wife gave him head—what I was talking about just now—while he was dying in the midday sun. She was taking it up the arse too, by the Romans that hung him, so I thought we could do the same. I could hang you by that rather large cross over there and we could take turns sucking and fucking you. Like everyone joining in. What do you say?"

A stunned silence in the church was almost audible. No one moved, no one said a thing, all staring at Michael in horror and disbelief. There had to be at least twenty people sitting there and all were paralysed with shock.

"See, it says something in the bible about love thy neighbour, literally, so what better way to do so than show that love in its physical form? By fucking? We can show God how much we love each other. Terence showed us how much love he had in his body. I know, I fucking drained it from him. Let's all fuck."

At the back of the church one of the parishioners rose and headed towards the door, perhaps sensing something was very wrong and potentially dangerous. She tried to open the door but Michael had already locked them mentally. No one was getting out of here until he was finished. And even then…

76

Realising that she was locked in, panic overcame her and she turned and screamed to be let out, banging on the door with her fists. This abruptly brought everyone else to their senses and they all jumped up and made a stampede towards the exit. All except Harry who was still in shock, staring at Michael as though he recognised him.

"Hi, Harry. I told you we were having fun that day. You should have joined us. Would have made a pleasant change from fucking your choir boys. Where are they today anyway?"

Harry gasped and backed away. "You. No. It can't be. You can't come in here. This is a holy place, a place of worship. Your presence is forbidden."

"Who said I can't worship as well? Been worshipping all my life, priest. And now you are all going to worship me."

Everyone was screaming and shouting now, trying to open the doors. They screamed even harder as he rose into the air, arms outstretched and his clothes magically fell away, leaving him naked and with his trusty hard-on. Harry held out his cross, surely knowing it made no difference. With a sweeping of his arm, he sent Harry flying back onto the large, wooden crucifix that covered almost the whole wall behind the altar. He was held there fast, replicating the figure of Jesus, arms outstretched too, moaning and whimpering.

His mental abilities now stronger than ever, he bade everyone to freeze and be quiet. They were under his control now, resistance impossible. God Himself might have made an appearance and He would have had trouble breaking Asmodeus' grip on them.

"Everyone get undressed," he barked.

They did so without question. Within seconds they were all naked except Harry, still pinned to the cross in his robe.

"Now, here's the thing. I call it hypocrisy. God banished us from heaven 'cause He didn't like what we were doing and suggesting, then what happens? He puts these two folks on Earth—naked, I should point out—and leaves them to fuck each other in Eden, in public. Can you believe that? Then, on top of that, His son is born here and shacks up with a prostitute of all people, a real, dirty one as well. I could tell you some stories about *that* girl you wouldn't believe, but anyway, now everyone talks about fuckin' as though it was a sin! Where did it all go wrong, I ask you? That guy up there on the cross, not Reverend Wilson who prefers the company of his choir boys, but the other one, he's going around with a *prostitute*. Tell me if that's not hypocrisy. I wanna hear it."

But no one did. They weren't even listening it seemed, screaming and shouting and begging for help. And it was pissing him off.

"So here's what we're gonna do. We're gonna teach your God that He got it all wrong. We, the ones He banished, are who were right all along and He didn't have the balls to admit it. Where I come from we do things how they were meant to be, embracing the good things in life and so today we're all gonna embrace Reverend Harry Wilson over there. That's fair, wouldn't you say, Harry?"

"Blasphemer. Snake. Go back to your foul land, serpent. You speak nothing but lies."

Harry slowly slid down the cross. The demon floated over to him and tore off his robe and the rest of his

78

clothes, Harry paralysed, unable to react.

"On the altar, please, Harry. Spread 'em nice and wide."

Harry cried out when he found himself walking over to the alter as if guided by unseen forces. When he reached the altar, he bent over so his hairy, scabby arse was on full display.

"That how you have the choir boys, Harry? Lining up, perhaps? Waitin' for their turn?"

"Be gone! Liar! I would never hurt God's children."

Asmodeus turned to all the parishioners, frozen in place like Harry but still retaining their voice. He stopped that too; they were going to attract unwelcome attention if not. "Now, would you please form a line and come on up. Quickly now."

They did as they were told, acting as though hypnotised. Which they technically were. When they reached a whimpering, sobbing Harry, Asmodeus approached the first man, an elderly guy in his sixties, perhaps. He rubbed a hand over his cock which stiffened instantly.

"Fuck him. Show him what God's love is all about."

Without debate, the man headed to Harry and sank his cock in his arse. Harry howled. Without lubrication it was probably quite painful, Asmodeus had to admit. Too late for that now, though.

"Good. Now in the meantime, I'd like you all to fuck each other. You can all take turns fucking Harry as each comes. Then repeat."

They did so. The church was now a mass orgy. Women and men fucking other. Some of the women were quite enterprising and were ramming their hands or fingers into other women's and men's arseholes and pussies; no judgement or discrimination here. When the elderly guy finally came inside Harry, he left and another replaced him. Immediately, the elderly guy started fucking some woman writhing on the floor with another.

It was music to the demon's ears, listening to their groaning and panting, the slapping of balls as they pounded each other that sounded like a crowd clapping, Harry crying and begging for help from God and anyone else who might have been listening.

"You watching this, God?" he yelled, looking up at the ceiling. "Whadaya think? Your son and his prostitute girlfriend woulda been proud! Come and join us. I'll fuck you myself!"

The floor was now beginning to get slippery with accumulated amounts of sweat and cum. Harry looked to be on the verge of passing out, cum and blood running in copious amounts down the back of his legs. Asmodeus was horny as fuck as well, so when the last guy came in Harry, he decided it was his turn.

"You're really slippery now, eh, Harry! Now you know how your choir boys felt. Like you even care, you dirty, perverted old fuck. You dare to stand up here and preach good and love, you make even me sick." He thrust into him hard. Something broke inside Harry's body. A rib maybe. He gripped Harry's sides with his hands, talons sinking into the soft flesh. He could feel an organ or two in there which he tickled, while fucking him as hard as he possibly could, Harry's roars of pain like thunder. Eventually, Asmodeus came inside him, while his fingers punctured holes in his stomach.

When he pulled out, automatically another man came to take his place. Asmodeus called another four over.

"Fuck him there as well."

They did as they were told, forcing their cocks into the holes made by his fingers. Now there were five banging into him from all angles while Jesus looked down from the cross behind them. Every time one of the men came, they immediately went and found another woman or man to replace the previous. Soon, it was blood that was running from their overworked cocks.

He let them continue for another hour or so. By this time every man in the church had had his turn with Harry at least once, others more, until he was barely conscious, a great pool of blood on the floor beneath him.

"Okay, folks, that's enough, I think. How did it feel, Harry? Are you feeling God's love now? Can you understand what it says now in the bible about love thy neighbour?"

But Harry could barely speak. His eyes were half closed and incoherent mumbling came from his lips.

"Oh well, never mind, soon be over. Now, one of the most important moments in the bible is the last supper. The feast before Jesus was taken. I think it was a form of bonding, letting them know what he was prepared to do in order to save his flock. I think it would be fitting we do the same.

"Folks, it's dinner time. His blood is your wine; his flesh your bread. Tuck in."

Asmodeus picked up Harry and threw him into the masses. Before he even hit the floor they lunged. Twenty mouths tore at the flesh on his body, multiple fingers raked and scratched at his skin trying to tear off parts of his body like a pack of wolves. One elderly woman, who an hour ago had required the use of a walking stick, now had Harry's cock in her mouth and was chewing on it, slavering and almost growling as another tried to push her off. One woman sank long, red fingernails into one of Harry's eyes and pulled it out with a plop. She swallowed it without even chewing. Then did the same with the other. A tug-of-war seemed to be happening over Harry's tongue. One man trying to wrench it free while another had his teeth clamped on it. It was torn in half, both lucky winners. Where Asmodeus had sunk his fingers into Harry's stomach others were doing the same, by now the gaps big enough to sink their whole hands in. They fumbled around for his organs and intestines and pulled them out through the holes.

It continued this way for another twenty minutes until all that was left of Harry was his skeleton. Even his skull had been stamped upon and crushed so they could get to the brain. Now, all twenty parishioners sat there panting, blood and guts and brain matter staining their faces and chests. They reminded Asmodeus of a pack of lions after a feast.

His job was done. He had used the boy to teach his parents what love really meant and he had taught Terence and Harry what worship was really all about. If God was watching the spectacle right now, Asmodeus thought He should be proud of him single-handedly spreading the word, what the bible was really about. Hypocrisy, that was what life here on Earth was all about and it made him sick. So much so it was time for him to teach the real message. He ordered his new parishioners to go get cleaned up and showered but not before disposing of Harry in the basement. Then, he would send one of them to buy clothes for all. It wouldn't look good to have his new flock wandering around the streets naked. People would think they were some weird, hippy cult or something. No, not good at all. In the meantime, Asmodeus donned Harry's old clothes and robe and winked up at Jesus on the cross.

"Let's have some fun, shall we, whadaya say?"

The End

I hope you enjoyed this dark tale. If so, please remember to leave a review on Amazon/Godless!

Sign up for my newsletter and grab your free book!

https://dl.bookfunnel.com/b00dfjcobx

Also by J. Boote

Man's Best Friend (on Amazon and Godless)

Also by Justin Boote

Novels:

Serial
Carnivore
The Ghosts of Northgate
A Mad World

Short Story Collections:

Love Wanes, Fear is Forever
Love Wanes, Fear is Forever: Volume 2
Love Wanes, fear is Forever: Volume 3

The Undead Possession series of novels:

Book 1: Infestation
Book 2: Resurrection
Book 3: Corruption
Book 4: Legion
Book 5: Resurgence

Short stories (on Godless.com)

If Flies Could Fart
Grandma Drinks Blood
Badass
A Question of Possession

Printed in Great Britain
by Amazon